para Yolanda, con todo mi corazón

FEATHERED SERPENT AND THE FIVE SUNS

A Mesoamerican Creation Myth

DUNCAN TONATIUH

Abrams Books for Young Readers • New York

It is said by the elders that before our time there were four other *tonatiuh*s or suns.

During the first tonatiuh, the gods created humans by covering sacred bones with mud.

The humans they made were big. They were giants! But they were clumsy. They would fall and break. These humans turned into mountains.

During the second tonatiuh, the gods made humans with mud again.

This time they made them small. But the mud would slip off their bones and slide into the rivers and lakes. These humans turned into fish.

During the third tonatiuh, the gods made humans by covering the sacred bones with corn paste instead of mud.

The humans they made were the right size and shape. But they refused to honor the gods. The gods became angry and turned these humans into monkeys that lived in trees.

During the fourth tonatiuh, the gods created humans with corn paste again.

This time, they gave the humans hearts. The humans they made were kind and honored the gods. But they were lazy. They did not want to hunt or grow food. They spent all day singing and playing. The gods turned these humans into birds.

The gods were tired. They did not want to create humans anymore. They gave the sacred bones to *Mictlantecuhtli*, the lord of the underworld, to keep.

But *Quetzalcóatl*—Feathered Serpent—the god of knowledge, did not want to give up.

I will travel to Mictlán—to the underworld—to recover the bones. I will create humans one last time, he thought.

He gathered his staff, his shield, his cloak, and his shell ornament for good luck and set off.

The entrance to Mictlán was in a cavern past the sacred mountains. There were nine regions Feathered Serpent would have to cross in order to reach the place where the lord of the underworld dwelled.

The first region was *Itzcuintlán*, the place where the dog lives. There Feathered Serpent encountered *Xólotl*, a spirit guide who helped those who were worthy of his aid.

The god had to cross a large and mighty river. *How will I reach the other side?*
he thought. But Xólotl motioned for him to climb onto his back and the dog carried
Feathered Serpent across the water.

The second region was *Tepeme Monamictlán*,
where mountains crashed into one another.

"How will I pass safely between them?"
Feathered Serpent wondered aloud.

He placed his staff between two mountains. This held them
back, and he and Xólotl passed through without harm.

He then reached *Itztépetl*, the obsidian mountain. Sharp volcanic glass shards cut anyone who tried to walk on them.

But Feathered Serpent tied rocks to the bottom of his sandals. "This should protect me," he said to Xólotl. The god crossed the mountain without getting hurt.

Then came *Cehuelóyan*, the place where it snows. Everything was frozen.

Feathered Serpent wrapped his *tilmatli* tightly around himself. The cloak was made from a special fabric. Despite the snow and ice, Feathered Serpent stayed warm and walked to the other side.

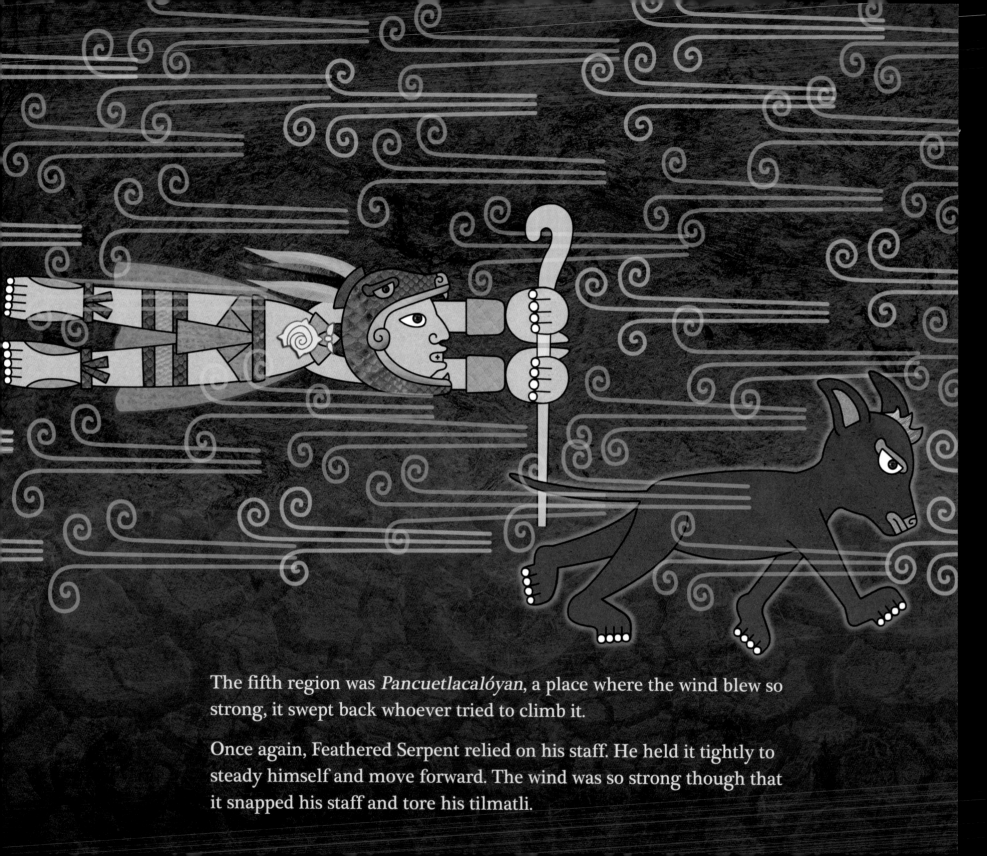

The fifth region was *Pancuetlacalóyan*, a place where the wind blew so strong, it swept back whoever tried to climb it.

Once again, Feathered Serpent relied on his staff. He held it tightly to steady himself and move forward. The wind was so strong though that it snapped his staff and tore his tilmatli.

The god then reached *Temiminalóyan*, the field where it rains arrows.

Feathered Serpent held his *chimalli* over his head. He was able to pass through unharmed, but his shield was broken in half by the sharp weapons.

The next region was *Teyollocualóyan*. It was a place where ferocious jaguars lived. "We are going to eat your heart!" they howled at Quetzalcóatl.

"You want my heart? Here. You can have it!" said the god. He dug his hand underneath his breastplate and then threw what was underneath to the jaguars.

The jaguars dashed for it. When they took a mighty bite, they broke their teeth! It was not his heart the god had thrown, but his shell ornament.

Afterward, Feathered Serpent reached *Apanohualóyan,* a place where the god had to cross a river again. Beneath the water dwelled a large reptile.

Feathered Serpent and Xólotl had to be careful not to disturb it as they swam across.

Feathered Serpent was now in the ninth region, *Chiconahualóyan*.
It was an area with nine bodies of water and a very dense fog.

"I can't even see my hands," exclaimed Feathered Serpent.
"How will I ever find my way?" But the god closed his eyes.
He became still and listened to Xólotl's breathing. The spirit
dog knew the way, and the god followed him.

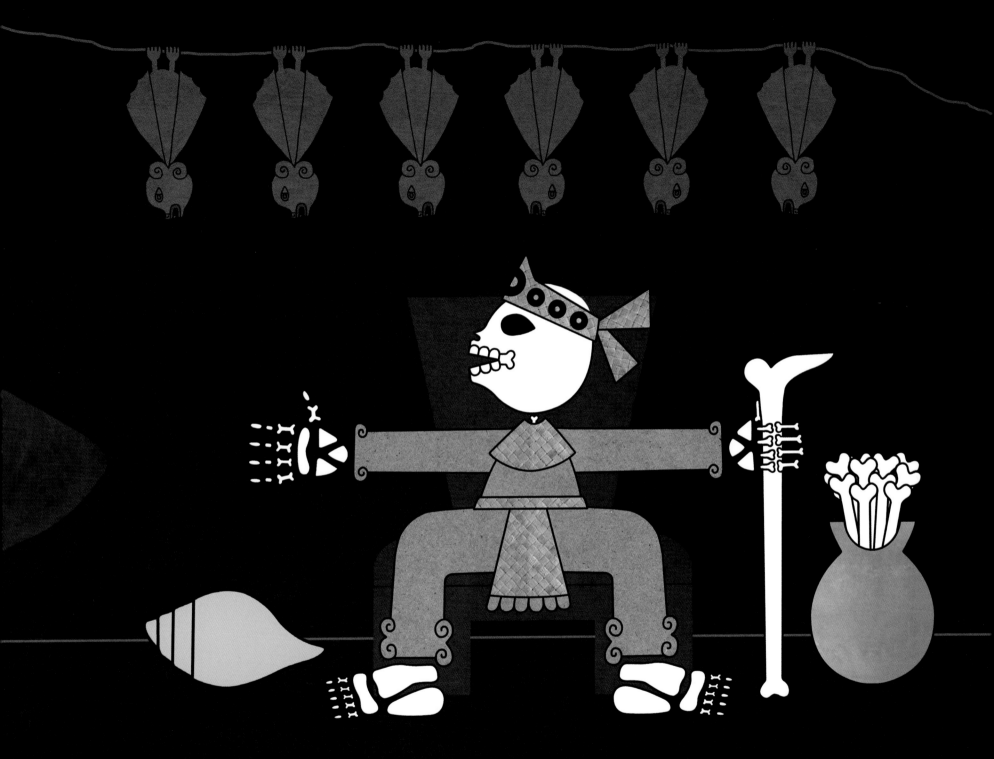

The fog dissipated. Feathered Serpent was finally in front of the god of the underworld.
"I am here to take the sacred bones. I want to bring humans to life," he said.

"You have come from far away and you have overcome many challenges, Feathered Serpent. But before you take the bones, you must pass one final test," said Mictlantecuhtli. "Take this shell and make music with it."

That is easy, thought the god. *All I have to do is blow.*

But when he took the shell from Mictlantecuhtli, he realized it was a trick! The shell did not have a hole to blow through.

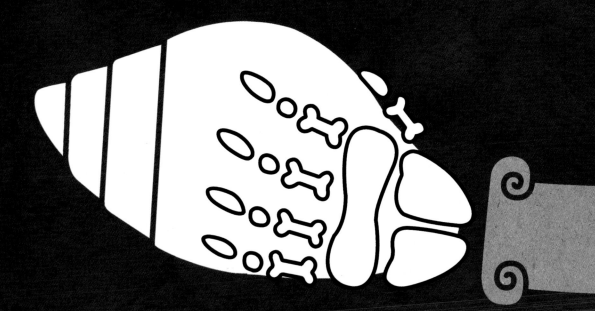

Feathered Serpent was not ready to give up, though. He saw some worms on the ground. He picked them up and placed them on the shell. The worms dug a hole in it. Feathered Serpent took a deep breath and blew. When he did, the instrument made powerful music.

Mictlantecuhtli was reluctant, but he gave Feathered Serpent the sacred bones. The god of knowledge knew he could not trust the god of the underworld, so he asked Xólotl, the spirit dog, to distract Mictlantecuhtli while he escaped.

Mictlantecuhtli soon realized that Feathered Serpent was getting away. "Stop him!" he yelled to the bats in his cave. The god ran and tried to shoo the creatures away. But while doing so, he failed to see a large hole in front of him. *Thump!!!* The god fell in. It was the end of Feathered Serpent and the sacred bones. Or so thought the lord of the underworld . . .

When Feathered Serpent woke up, he was bleeding and terribly hurt. He collected the broken sacred bones. He climbed out of the hole and made the journey out of Mictlán.

He then went to the place where the other gods dwelled. He smashed the bones into a powder and mixed some of his own blood with it. He asked the other gods to do the same. With the powder and the blood, Feathered Serpent made a paste, and with the paste, the gods made humans again.

It is said by the elders that we are the descendants of those humans and that we are living in the fifth tonatiuh.

AUTHOR'S NOTE

The feathered serpent is a symbol that appears prominently and often in the temples, sculptures, murals, artifacts, and codices of many Mesoamerican civilizations. The first known depiction of a feathered serpent in the Americas is in a stone monument that is more than 2,500 years old. It was created by the Olmecs, and it is in an archaeological site named *La Venta*, in the present-day Mexican state of Tabasco. Other depictions have been found in archaeological sites like Teotihuacán, Xochicalco, Chichén Itzá, and Tenochtitlán—which are the remains of cities built by the Toltecs, the Mayans, and the Aztecs.

It can be challenging to understand who or what the feathered serpent was. When the Spanish and other Europeans came to this continent, they destroyed the temples and codices of the indigenous people because they did not resemble their own beliefs and customs. The knowledge we have of the feathered serpent comes from interpreting the depictions that have survived. It also comes from the writing of Spanish friars, such as Fray Bernardino de Sahagún, who soon after the conquest sought to learn about the beliefs of the indigenous people instead of destroying them.

Nahuatl-speaking cultures knew the feathered serpent as Quetzalcóatl. In the Nahuatl language, *quetzal* means "precious feather" and *cóatl* means "snake." To them, feathered serpent wasn't just a god, but also a historical figure—an actual Toltec priest-king who lived in the tenth century and whose full name was Ce Acatl Topiltzin Quetzalcóatl. The stories and attributes of feathered serpent the god and of feathered serpent the king are often tangled together.

To the Aztecs, Quetzalcóatl was one of the main gods. He was the god of knowledge; the patron of arts and crafts. He was associated with the wind and is sometimes depicted wearing a birdlike mouthpiece. He was also associated with the planet Venus—which shines like a star in the sky. Xólotl, the god of dusk and twins, was also associated with Venus. He was considered feathered serpent's *nahual*, a kind of animal twin spirit. Quetzalcóatl is the protagonist of several important myths, including the creation of the world and the creation of man. He is also credited with giving corn and the maguey plant to humans. Corn was the main staple in the Mesoamerican diet, and maguey was very important for ceremonial purposes.

In this book, I focus on the myth of the five suns. There are different versions of the story. It is mentioned in codices and it also appears in the chronicles of indigenous people, who sought to preserve some of their beliefs in writing soon after they were colonized. The version I tell is based on a Cuauhtitlán chronicle. The encounter between Quetzalcóatl and Mictlantecuhtli is shown prominently in both images and writings, but not much is shown of Quetzalcóatl's journey through Mictlán.

The Aztecs believed that when people died, they went to one of four places. Warriors who died in battle, those who were sacrificed, and women who died giving birth went to the house of the sun. People who drowned or died because of water went to an evergreen paradise named *Tlalocan*. Children who died before they were born went to a place where a tree nursed them so they could be born again in the future. All others went to Mictlán.

The Aztecs believed the journey to the final region of the underworld—where the dead's spirit could finally find rest—took four years, which is approximately the time that it takes a corpse to decompose and become a skeleton. In this book, I imagined how Quetzalcóatl would have confronted the arduous journey through the regions of Mictlán. I created this version of "Feathered Serpent and the Five Suns" to celebrate the mythology of Mesoamerica and to introduce young readers to this rich tradition.

GLOSSARY

Most of the words I include here are in Nahuatl, the language spoken by the Aztecs and by other Mesoamerican cultures from the central region of Mexico. Some indigenous groups still speak Nahuatl. Many words of Nahuatl origin have become part of Spanish as it is spoken nowadays.

APANOHUALÓYAN (ah-pan-oh-wal-OH-yan): place where you have to cross water

CEHUELÓYAN (seh-well-OH-yan): place with much snow

CHICONAHUALÓYAN (chee-con-ah-wal-OH-yan): Place where there are nine waters. This was the last region of Mictlán. The dead had to cross through a dense fog before they reached Mictlantecuhtli.

CHIMALLI (CHEE-mah-lee): shield

ITZCUINTLÁN (eetz-queen-TLAN): place of the dog

ITZTÉPETL (its-TEH-petl): obsidian mountain

MESOAMERICA: The term refers to a geographic area during a specific period of time. Mesoamerica extended from what is now central Mexico in the north to what is now Costa Rica in the south. It lasted from approximately 1,000 years BC until the colonization of the region by the Spanish in the sixteenth century. Different Mesoamerican civilizations rose and fell; among them were the Olmecs, Toltecs, Mayas, Mixtecs, Zapotecs, and Aztecs. They shared similarities in their beliefs, art, architecture, and technology.

MICTLÁN (meek-TLAN): the underworld

MICTLANTECUHTLI (meek-TLAN-teh-koo-tlee): god of the dead, lord of the underworld

MYTH: A story that explains a natural or social phenomenon such as the creation of the world or the creation of humans. It often involves supernatural beings or events.

PANCUETLACALÓYAN (pan-qwet-lack-ah-LOH-yan): Place where people turn like a flag. The strong winds in this region of Mictlán made those who crossed it fly in the air like a flag or a kite.

QUETZALCÓATL (ket-sal-KOH-atl): *Quetzal* means "precious feather" and *cóatl* means "snake." The feathered serpent was one of the primary gods for many Mesoamerican civilizations.

TEMIMINALÓYAN (teh-meem-meen-ah-LOH-yan): place where arrows are shot

TEPEME MONAMICTLÁN (TEH-peh-meh moh-nam-meek-TLAN): place where the mountains meet

TEYOLLOCUALÓYAN (teh-yo-yo-qwa-LOH-yan): place where they eat your heart

TILMATLI (teel-MAH-tlee): An outer garment used by men, similar to a cape.

TONATIUH (TOH-nah-tee-oo): sun or sun god

XÓLOTL (SHOL-otl): He was considered by the Aztecs and Toltecs to be the god of dusk and of twins. He was depicted like a xoloitzcuintli, which is a breed of hairless dog native to Mesoamerica.

SELECTED BIBLIOGRAPHY

Amlin, Patricia. *The Five Suns: A Sacred History of Mexico.* Berkeley, CA: Berkeley Media LLC, 1996.

Anders, Ferdinand, Maarten Jansen, and Luis Reyes García. *Religión, costumbres e historia de los antiguos mexicanos: libro explicativo del llamado códice Vaticano A.* Mexico City: Fondo de Cultura Económica, 1996.

Baldwin, Neil. *Legends of the Plumed Serpent: Biography of a Mexican God.* New York: PublicAffairs, 1998.

Barbeytia, Luis. *Mito, leyenda e historia de Quetzalcóatl, la misteriosa Serpiente Emplumada.* Mexico City: CIDCLI, 2015.

León-Portilla, Miguel. *Los antiguos mexicanos a través de sus crónicas y cantares.* Mexico City: Fondo de Cultura Económica, 1961.

Rius. *Quetzalcóatl no era del PRI.* Mexico City: Grijalbo, 1987.

Saenz, Cesar A. *Quetzalcoatl.* Mexico City: Instituto Nacional de Antropología e Historia, 1962.

The art in this book was hand drawn then collaged digitally.

Cataloging-in-Publication Data has been applied for and may be obtained from the Library of Congress.

ISBN 978-1-4197-4677-2

Text and illustrations copyright © 2020 Duncan Tonatiuh
Edited by Howard W. Reeves
Book design by Steph Stilwell and Heather Kelly

Printed and bound in China
10 9 8 7 6 5 4 3

Abrams Books for Young Readers are available at special discounts when purchased in quantity for premiums and promotions as well as fundraising or educational use. Special editions can also be created to specification. For details, contact specialsales@abramsbooks.com or the address below.

Abrams® is a registered trademark of Harry N. Abrams, Inc.

ABRAMS The Art of Books
195 Broadway, New York, NY 10007
abramsbooks.com

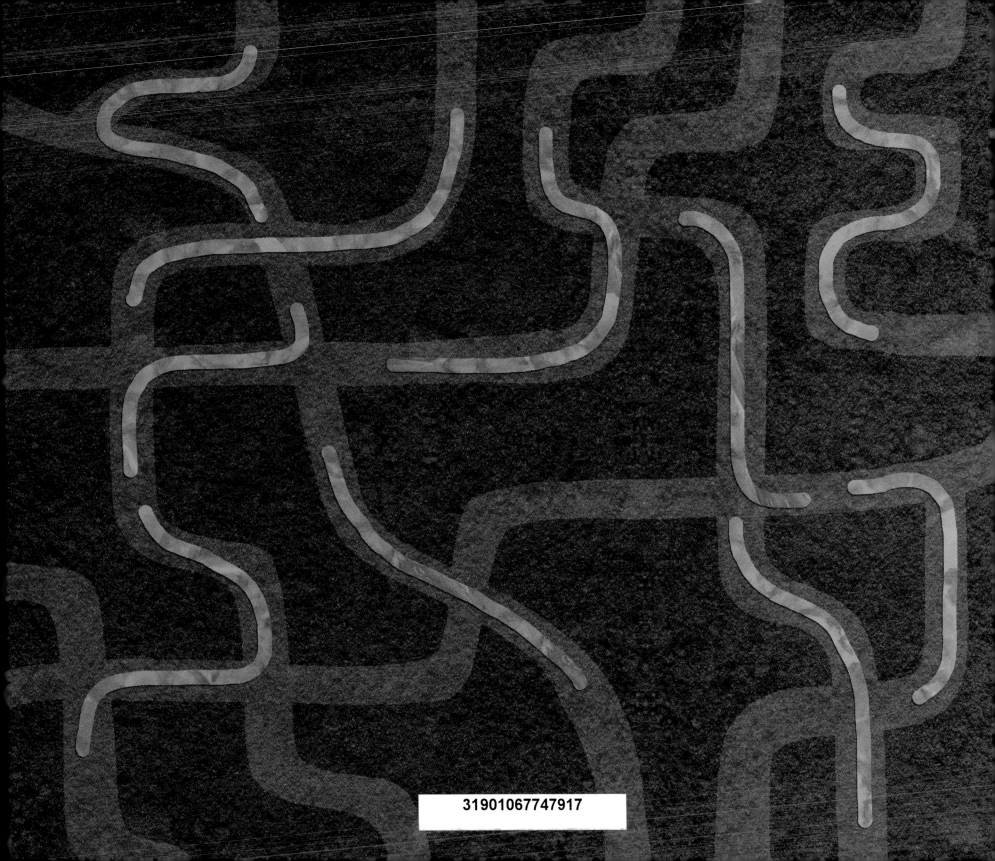